Red Christmas

Disturbing yuletide tales for grown-ups

Michael Wombat

Also by Michael Wombat

NOVELS & NOVELLAS
Warren Peace
Fog
Moth Girl versus The Bats
Tooth and Claw
Crow
The Raven's Wing

SHORT STORY COLLECTIONS
Blood on the Ground
The Museum of White Walls
M. Monvoisin's Emporium of Extraordinary Adventures
Red Christmas

AS EDITOR AND CONTRIBUTOR
Soul of the Universe
Cutthroats & Curses
Human 76

ESSAYS AND ARTICLES
Cubic Scats

WOMBAT IN MY POCKET
1. A Pocketful of Surprises
2. A Pocketful of Wonders
3. A Pocketful of Stardust
4. A Pocketful of Whispers
5. A Pocketful of Wry

Patrons

A huge thank you, as ever, to my patrons:

> Kiera Bruce
> Gaudi Daamen
> Lotte D'Hulster
> Steve Hutchings
> Sheilagh Johnson
> Karel Karezman
> Stephen Leatherdale
> Catherine Rowley-Williams
> Lynette Sherburne
> Jaime Smith
> Julie Sorrell
> The Endless Knot
> A mysterious gentleman of the shadows

If you have a hankering to join that merry band in supporting my writing — and, incidentally, seeing exclusive patrons-only stories and other goodies — then please visit my Patreon page at https://www.patreon.com/wombat37.

Contents

Aschenputtel

"For you, Mama."

Her mother had always taught Aschenputtel to be honest and humble and true, and she tried to show her gratitude by visiting the grave whenever she could slip away. The marigolds brightened the small headstone, half hidden by ivy, a smudge of gold in the monochrome predawn, dusted white by December's gown.

Aschenputtel stood and turned. A small bird chirruped from the tree above, the first of the chorus. She looked back down to the ancient, crumbling stone house. It squatted below the hill like a fat toad. They would be awake down there in an hour. Beautiful to the eye they were, but their hearts were ugly-foul and black. If a fire was not already burning in the grate when they arose, they would punish her once more. She plucked a burdock leaf and rubbed it gently on the half-healed, burned skin of her forearm.

A flicker caught her eye. An ochre mote blinked in the near distance. It was a light, buttercup yellow, bobbing along the track through the frost-dressed wood, flickering through the dark tree trunks. It came accompanied by a growing sound, all rattles and jingles and a thump of hooves. A carriage, pulled by two white horses, emerged from the trees and swept to a halt in front of the house. The driver jumped down and banged on the front door. A second figure seemed almost to glide from the carriage after the first, who once again thumped the door with mighty force.

She would have work, if there were visitors. Her rough wooden shoes picked a careful way down the precipitous path that wound down the hill. Voices from below welcomed the surprise guests, with first anger, then a tone of query, surprise, and, oddly, effusive welcome. It was not like her father to welcome anyone, let alone with enthusiasm. The dawn visitors must be special indeed.

The sky paled. She slid down the last few feet on her backside, dirtying further her filthy, brown smock. She tried to open the back door silently, but it could not resist a throaty creak. She paused, holding it ajar. Voices rang inside.

"… also is not the right one," a man said. "I can see the blood where your daughter has disfigured her foot to make it fit!"

"I assure you—" Her father's voice, cut off.

"Have you no other daughter?"

"No, sir. But ... perhaps if you were able to describe the girl in question, I would know her?"

"As you well know, man, it was a masked ball. Masked."

"Aschenputtel!!" The screech made her jump. The door slipped from her fingers and swung wide. Her father and his wife stood with a man in a dark cloak, who sported an impossibly wide moustache. He held a small object that glinted in the candlelight. A second stranger sat at the table, his face hidden beneath a hood.

"Why lurk you there, wretch?" her step-mother snapped. "Make haste and light a fire! Our guests are cold!"

Aschenputtel scurried to the hearth, and lifted two logs onto the grate. Her fingers shook as she separated enough kindling to take a spark. She would pay for this later with a beating.

"Chamberlain?" A new voice, a liquid purr.

"Yes, sire? Oh! Are you sure? She's filthy. Her arse is caked with, well, who knows what?"

"This girl?" laughed her father. "This stunted scullion was left behind when my first wife croaked. She cannot be the one you are looking for. As you see, she never bathes, and you can likely smell her across the room."

"Nevertheless." That purr again from within the hood, soft like a warm hug on a cold night.

"But she never leaves the house! Last night she was here, sleeping on this very floor—"

"Be silent, man. Chamberlain?"

"My lady, if you please?"

Aschenputtel felt a hand on her shoulder. My lady? Did he mean her? Her fingers shook, and she dropped the kindling. She kept her grimy face lowered, but turned her eyes up. The chamberlain took her arm and helped her to her feet. She wondered how he managed to make his whiskers project horizontally fully two inches past his cheeks.

"Will you sit?"

He gestured to a stool, and she warily eased her buttocks onto the hard seat, aware of the dampness of her mud-caked smock beneath her. The moustachioed man swung his long cloak behind him with an elegant movement, and knelt at her feet. Her mouth gaped as he drew her foot out of its heavy wooden shoe. A rich stench wafted from her feet, and she lowered her head in shame, but the chamberlain seemed not to notice. The thing that he held glinted as, with cool fingers, he slid it over her foot. It was a golden, filigree slipper, a little blood-stained at the toe. The tips of the man's moustache twitched upwards as he grinned. He stood, helping her to her feet.

"It fits!" he laughed. "It fits perfectly, sire!"

The man at the table crossed to face her, and shook off his hood. He was beautiful.

"It's you, isn't it?" His voice caressed her ears. She said nothing. "You came secretly to the ball last night, and you danced with me."

Aschenputtel frowned. She had, as her father had said, slept through the night on the kitchen floor, left alone when the others had gone out in their finery.

"We kissed in the garden, you and I," the handsome man continued. He reached up and took a twig of myrtle from her hair. "I fell in love with you at that moment. When you ran, you left behind your golden slipper."

She had never in her life even seen such a slipper, nor ever a man as handsome as this.

"I knew I could use it to find you, for no other's foot would fit so dainty a shoe. And I was right, was I not?"

She stared at him, wide-eyed.

"Will you marry me? Be my princess and live at the palace with me?" A small frown wrinkled his brow. "It *is* you, isn't it? You did dance and kiss and sing with me at the ball last night?"

Her mother had always taught her to be honest and humble and true, but where had that taken her? To a life of filth and servitude, a misery of existence. For the first time in her life, Aschenputtel lied.

"Yes," she said. "It's me. I danced with you. I kissed you. We sang. Take me away from this shithole."

A Christmas Gift

My Own Edith,

I don't know how properly to start this letter. The circumstances are different from any under which I ever wrote before. I won't post it for now but will keep it in my pocket. I write these words on Boxing Day. I never imagined, when this damned war began, that I would still be separated from my sweetheart at Christmas. I miss your voice, your smiling eyes.

We go over the top soon. If the worst happens perhaps someone will post this. If I survive, I will post it to you myself with kisses added. Lieutenant Reith should by rights censor our letters, but I'm told that he hasn't the heart for it, and I'm hopeful that it will one day reach you intact.

I have your latest letter here; a ray of light in a filthy world. I'm very glad to discover that you appreciate Cornish pasties. So do I, and often eat a hot one when on my way back from town. Can you fancy me climbing the hill, cane in one hand and a hot pasty in the other? Quite a study for one of your snapshots! I look forward to a lifetime finding out more things about you.

Thank you for the socks. They were most welcome. You cannot imagine how awful are the conditions here. The freezing trench is filled with mud, ordure to the knees, worse things that I cannot describe to a lady. One pair of socks kept my feet warm as intended, while the second served well as gloves as I stood watch on Christmas Eve.

I was on the firing step, trying to keep warm, listening to Ames' gramophone recording of *"Roses of Picardy"* playing repeatedly. When it ended for the hundredth time, I heard other music in the frosty air. I heard singing from the Hun lines: "*Stille Nacht*". Keeping low, I glanced over. There were lighted candles along the lip of the Hun trench, exceedingly pretty in the frosty night. As the carol ended a guttural cry went up.

"English soldier! English soldier! A merry Christmas!"

The Bosche were calling to us. I could not help myself, and answered.

"*Glücklich Weihnachten* to you too, Fritz!" I shouted, hoping my schoolboy German was correct.

"You sing now, Tommy!" one of them laughed, and sing we did. Through the night we exchanged songs, then came the dawn, pencilling the sky with grey and pink, heralding another day of pointless slaughter.

I peered over the wall, my hand gripping my rifle, and my eyes widened. Some ten feet above no-man's land hovered a strange glowing light, bright in the approaching dawn. It twinkled and shone. No flare this, for it hung motionless, a pure radiance. I reminded me of, well, a star.

You must understand, darling, what living with constant death and dismemberment does to a man. It makes him to fear nothing if he knows that at any moment he may be blown to smithereens. I laid down my rifle and set my foot on the wooden ladder.

"Private Fulton, do not respond!" hissed Lieutenant Reith, "It's a Bosche trick!"

I ignored Lieutenant Reith and clambered out of the trench. I stumbled over the rutted mud towards the beautiful light. As I reached it, it faded and disappeared and I looked down in disappointment. In a crater at my feet lay perhaps a dozen dead Germans. I then realised one of them was moving, and moaning softly.

"Tommy! Merry Christmas! We come to meet the brave man who greets us! We have wine! Will you share with us?" I looked up to see four Hun walking nervously towards me, arms out, carrying bottles. They were smiling broadly. Were these the savage, brutal barbarians that we had been told about?

"You have a wounded man here!" I beckoned to the approaching Saxons, "*Schnell! Schnell!*"

The Germans hurried to carry to safety their wounded comrade, one Otto Dix apparently. I do hope he survives. Soldiers from both sides wandered out to join us and we commenced to talk, to laugh. The Germans were not at all evil. They were very decent chaps.

We exchanged cigarettes, chocolate, wine and stories. I showed one man your photograph. He declared you *'zehr schöne'*. He showed me a picture of his three young children, all of them with dark curls and happy smiles. We looked forward to a time when we could embrace our loved ones again.

All Christmas Day we relaxed, conversing and singing together, comrades in an unofficial truce and united in hatred for this bloody war. We wrote our names and addresses on field service postcards, and exchanged them for Bosche ones. We cut buttons off our coats and took in exchange the Imperial Arms of Germany. But our gift of gifts was Christmas pudding. The sight of it made the Germans' eyes grow wide with hungry wonder, and at the first bite they were our friends for ever.

At eight, Lieutenant Reith fired three shots in the air, put up a flag with *'Merry Christmas'* on it, and climbed on the high parapet. The Bosche raised a sheet with *'Danke'*, and the German Captain appeared also. These two bowed, saluted, then dropped into their respective trenches. The Hun fired two shots in the air, and the War was on again.

I don't think I will ever—

It is with real sorrow that I must add to this letter some very bad news about your fiancé, Private Michael Fulton. He played a very gallant part in the attack on the German position made by this regiment on 26th December, 1914. He helped his company commander to a place of safety after the former was wounded, but in doing so was hit by a shell fragment and died immediately. I cannot tell you how sorry I am. Everyone thought so much of him, and admired his fine sturdy character and unfailing cheerfulness.

He it was that led us to maintain the truce described above, and for the gift of peace he gave them on Christmas Day scores of men will be eternally grateful. Let pride then be mingled with your tears. May God comfort and console you.

Lt. John Reith, 8th King's Own Regt., BEF

Claustrophobia

Oh bum. How the jingle bells did this happen? Bloody centuries I've been doing this; how come all of a sudden I get stuck? I mean, yeah, in this dark I can see the sum total of sod all, but that's never stopped me before, even in really tight squeezes. The old Santa Wriggle usually gets me through any gap, as well as pleasing the elves at the Boxing Day Hullabaloo. Heh, it's all in the hips, you know.

It's become quite the dance at the party – great lines of elves and fairies, not to mention the missus, all doing the old Santa Wriggle. OK, yes, I call our celebration the Boxing Day Hullabaloo, and that's a British thing and I'm originally Dutch, but I just like that name, you know? Boxing Day – the day after Christmas according to the Brits. It trips off the tongue, don't you think? The Boxing Day Hullabaloo. Mind you, that won't be happening this year if I can't move myself.

The old Santa Wriggle is not doing it; not this sodding time. I can't shift, neither up nor down. I blame the missus' new mince pie recipe; the one with extra butter. I ate fifty yesterday. Might have gained a few inches, I suppose.

Bloody hell, it's pitch-black, my nose is pressed against filthy rotting bricks, I've got soot up my nose and I do *not* like it. I feel pressed in, squished tight. I might never get out, and then what? No more toys for good little girls and boys, no more coal for the naughty sods. It'll be a bloody disaster.

What's that, you say? Santa shouldn't swear? Piss off; you'd be letting out a non-stop stream of all the swears you know if you had to go through what I do once a year. Up and down all those sodding chimneys, and all within twenty-four hours? It's not bloody easy! Yes, yes, my time-slowing ability thingy helps, and that teleportation device that Elf Ansafety came up with proved invaluable when people started living places without chimneys. But you know, that's not the whole job, not by a long chalk.

Have you ever thought what happens when a reindeer decides to have a poo right up there on someone's roof? Of course you haven't, your minds are all full of tinsel and glitter at Christmas. Well let me tell you, you can't just leave it up there, it'd stink for days. And imagine the questions once it was found. Nope, Muggins here has to shovel it all up and put it in the poo sack. Think yourselves lucky I don't get *that* mixed up with the sack of toys. Ah well, at least the reindeer don't drop their *'doings'* in flight, cos that'd be a terrible Christmas present for anyone down below.

This isn't getting me shifted, is it? I feel all closed in, trapped, and I'm sure there's not enough air in here. And what the hell's that sharp thing sticking into my bloody arse? Come on, Nick, see if you can reach round to have a feel. Ah, loose brick. Maybe if I can wiggle it out... OUCH! No no, bad idea, bad idea. Better leave it. No one wants a sharp brick corner poking them up *there*. I'd better see if I can call that lazy cow of a fairy down here, see if she has any bright ideas. Maybe she can magic me free.

OI! NUFF, WHERE ARE YOU? GET DOWN HERE!

Bet she's sitting on Dasher's antlers having a right old gossip. What's the use of having a fairy PA if all she does is sit about swapping recipes and talking about soap operas with reindeer?

I bet my beard's as black as, well, soot by now. I probably look more like Brian Blessed than Sinterklaas. You don't know Brian? Give him a Google, then you'll know what I'm on about. Mind you, Brian wouldn't be up a chimney would he? Probably down the pub having a pint of ale, like a man with sense. Unlike me, with no sense, stuck up a chimney and probably never going to get out and I might stop breathing soon and oh no oh no...

NUFF, GET DOWN THIS CHIMNEY NOW OR I'LL STICK YOU ON THE TIPPY-TOP OF MY TREE NEXT YEAR!

Calm down, Nicky, calm down. Panic will do you no good at all. Maybe if I twist my arm like this – whoa, at least that dislodged something. I think I can get my fingers to it, I... *ew!* It's all bony and feathery and, *ew*, gooey. I think it's... *ugh*, dead bird, probably, and I poked my fingers into it. Ick ick ick.

NUFF! WHAT THE HELL ARE YOU PLAYING AT UP THERE? BRING YOUR WAND DOWN HERE THIS INSTANT, YOUNG FAIRY!

Bumholes, got a mouthful of grit there. Tastes like burnt - wait, what was that? I'm sure I heard something. Yes, there it is again. Noises beneath my boots. Sort of a scraping and a tapping. Is someone down there?

"Yes, ma'am, it is early! Never mind, I'll soon have the fire roaring and then the children can come down!"

Uh-oh.

Nativity

Miss Brightsmith smiled happily. This year's nativity play was going extremely well, a stark contrast to last year's disaster. Everything that could go wrong did go wrong last year. The baby Jesus losing his head, which rolled into the front row of the audience. The innkeeper saying to Mary and Joseph "Yes, come in, there's plenty of room." Worst of all, the Archangel suddenly getting severe stage fright and weeing himself before sitting down in the puddle and bawling his eyes out.

This year, however, the children were doing her proud. Kara James was word perfect as Mary, and her brother Ethan's Joseph, though snotty, was performing with a bravado that made the audience of indulgent Mums and Dads chuckle.

This year Miss Brightsmith had, for once, decided to take a seat in the audience rather than standing fretting in the wings, and it was paying dividends. Much of the tension was lifted out here among the smiling, Christmas-spirited adults perched awkwardly on chairs that were just too small. Here she was able to appreciate the play for what it was; a joyful slice of

Christmas fun presented by five-year-olds, rather than a professional production that had to be word-perfect.

"And lo a mighty star..." announced Lisa Shambrook, projecting her voice just as Miss Brightsmith had taught her. This was just perfect. As the youthful voices joined to sing '*Away in a Manger*', she looked about her. Most of the audience was beaming, eyes moist as their offspring sang to them the same song that they too had sung for their own parents decades ago.

Now that the play was nearing its end, several of the smallest children were becoming tired or bored. Shepherds fiddled with their trousers, stars waved to their mummies and sheep picked their noses. There only remained the crowning moment when the Archangel appears to bless everyone and to prompt the singing of the final carol. Following last year's disaster, Miss Brightsmith had decided to try something different this time. She had built a fairly high platform to the rear of the stage, unobtrusive until lit by a single spotlight. She had chosen the brightest boy in her class, the eager and enthusiastic Caleb Walker, as her Archangel. He had listened intently as she instructed him how to carefully climb the steps and step into the spotlight right on clue. She had impressed upon him the importance of his role, and he was determined to present the Archangel properly.

"Don't worry, Miss. I won't let you down," he had piped cheerily. "My Mam always says the show must go on."

"You should always listen to your Mam," she had smiled. "Be careful not to let go of the handrail when you're on the platform."

"I won't, Miss. I know the angel's important, and I know what to do. I'm not nervous or anything. The show must go on."

Caleb's moment had arrived. Right on cue, he appeared behind and above the assorted children on the stage. The audience gasped. The new arrangement had worked better than Miss Brightsmith could have dreamed. The Archangel seemed to materialise out of thin air, and he looked ethereal and translucent, glowing with light. His paper wings wafted gently, looking almost real. Caleb spoke his line with a meaning and conviction that belied his age.

"Joy to all here assembled! May everyone find true happiness and love through all their life. Harken to the heralds of peace!"

Everyone in the school hall joined in a rousing rendition of '*Hark The Herald Angels Sing*' as Caleb faded out of the spotlight and the hall lights came up. An enthusiastic round of applause filled the hall as the song ended. Afterwards, parents sought her out and congratulated her on the wonderful production.

"Miss Brightsmith?"

She turned round, beaming, ready to accept more praise, but her face adopted a puzzled expression when she saw that the man who had spoken was a serious-faced police constable, his hat gripped in his left hand.

"Yes?" she raised her eyebrows, "Can I help you?"

"It's about Caleb Walker, I'm afraid."

"Really? I can't imagine why you'd be interested in him. He's one of the good ones, never any trouble.. He'll be getting changed right now. I'll see if I can find him for you."

"I'm sorry," the constable laid a gentle hand on her arm. "Your Headmistress was supposed to have told you already, but apparently there was some sort of mix-up with the secretary not passing on a message. The Head only discovered that you hadn't heard a short time ago, when I arrived to make certain arrangements. Since I am trained in such matters, I offered to tell you the news myself."

"I don't understand."

"My apologies, I'll speak plainly. Caleb Walker was run down by a hit-and-run driver on his way to school this morning, and suffered massive head injuries. He was rushed to hospital, where the doctors did everything they could, but I am afraid he died from those injuries at about eight-thirty this morning."

"But—"

"I'm sorry that you weren't told. You must have been worried when he didn't turn up."

"I thought... I think he might have."

"Hmmm," the constable nodded, his expression a mix of confusion and concern, possibly for her state of mind. "I see that you managed to find a stand-in for your angel, anyway. The show must go on, eh?"

"Yes, yes. Bless him, Caleb was always determined that the show must go on."

Red Christmas

The pale skin resisted for one tantalising moment before parting under his assault. He dug deeper, searching for the pulsing vein, and grunted his satisfaction as it was pierced. He sucked greedily, and the hot blood coursed down his throat, new and fresh. It flowed easily, spilling from his lips and staining his whiskers. Above the usual iron tang, he could taste cinnamon and sugar. She'd been eating scones.

At most houses, of course, he simply collected the blood. Even his huge belly could not hold the blood of every child in the world. So he stored it, up in the ship – sorry, *sleigh* – taking a few drops from a slit made under the tongue with his fingernail. The amount taken was not enough to be noticed from a single child. When multiplied by the number of children in the world, however, there was more than enough to sustain him through the year. He drugged them first, of course. It would not do for them to waken during the process. A handful of – well, let's call it *Fairy Dust* – ensured that there would be no sudden nightmares for the little darlings.

This child though, oh this child he had not been able to resist. Tired and peckish after a long time-slowed night, he had been slow to sprinkle the *Dust*. She had been awake when he had arrived, face flooded with delight as Santa appeared in her bedroom, her wide blue eyes twinkling with life and surprise, blonde tresses framing a face full of joy. Her expression hadn't slipped as he threw himself at her and ripped the nightdress down over her shoulders, exposing her vibrant skin. His teeth ripped at her neck before the beatific smile had left her face.

It never ceased to amaze him, the blithe acceptance by humans of his existence, of his immortality. Their assumption that he was benign and loving. Did they never question how he managed to return, year after year, century after century, never aging? That they fell constantly for the smoke and mirrors of the merry outfit and the cheap gifts spoke volumes for their blinkered idiocy.

A rattling gasp close by his ear told him that she was close to death. Swiftly he drew his nail across his wrist, loosing his own blood. He pushed the girl's mouth against it. Her lips moved only slightly, sliding weakly against the bloody skin. She was almost gone. He had left it too late.

No, wait. She stirred, and her tongue slipped between her lips. She lapped at his blood, then sucked harder to draw more out of him. She was feeling The Thirst. His timing had been exquisite. He twisted his fingers in her hair and tore her away from him. She snarled and tried to bite him. He grabbed a mince pie left out for him, dipped it in her blood and crammed it into her gore-streaked mouth.

"Now, little girl, come with Santa. You'll enjoy being an elf. Ho ho ho!"

The Sledgehog

The snow-smothered landscape spun wildly, upside-down and dazzle-white. Gunnar closed his eyes, but that did not diminish either his dizziness or his terror. Mamma had warned him not to stray too far, but he had become fascinated by animal tracks in the snow.

One trail in particular had intrigued him – the footprint was long and narrow, with three toes pointing forwards, and two going out to the sides. They looked like the ones that Mamma had told him were hedgehog tracks, but these were far larger, from an animal more the size of Egill Jónsson's prize pig.

Gunnar had followed the footmarks much longer than he ought, winding and wandering the wood, hoping to catch sight of whatever creature had left the tracks. They led him to a patch of flattened snow, spattered with red. His mind had barely registered that this might be blood before he was swept off his feet, gripped by the ankles and borne away, head-down, through the frozen wood.

He tried to steady his whirling vision, and looked up past his feet, which were gripped tightly by a vast hand, bony-knuckled and hairy. He had been caught by some sort of monster, a giant dressed in rags and furs. He could see little but the leg against which he bumped as the creature loped through the forest.

"Boy!" A voice hissed.

"Hello," Gunnar said. "Who's there?"

"I'm on the other side of the monster. She holds me in her other hand," the voice said. "I too have been captured by Grýla."

"What is a Grýla?"

"She is a giant, a troll, a grim monster. She and her husband Leppalúði live in a cave at the foot of he mountain. Surely your mamma must have warned you about them?"

"No. But she did make me wear my new scarf, in case I met Jólakötturinn."

"The cat that eats anyone not wearing new clothing? Yes, he is Grýla's cat, and lives with her in her cave. I fear that is where she is taking us."

They left the trees, and began to climb uphill, towards the crags of the high mountain. As they lifted rhythmically by Gunnar's face, the troll's leather-wrapped feet gave off a stench that could not be masked by the cold.

"Why is she taking us to her cave?" Gunnar asked, his voice trembling.

"Grýla has an insatiable appetite for the flesh of all creatures, such as mischievous children and, well, me. She boils whatever she catches in a large pot. She is especially dangerous at this time of year, around Christmas-time, when her sons visit. They eat a lot, so she needs constantly to make stew for them to eat."

"Stew from us?"

"Yes, stew from us."

"But I don't want to be stew."

"Neither do I. What is your name?"

"Gunnar."

"I am Broddgöltur. And do not fear, Gunnar, for I have a plan."

The troll climbed higher, farting as she stretched her legs up the gradient, wrinkling Gunnar's nose even more. Swinging upside-down was giving him a headache, and he shivered from cold as well as fear. It was almost a relief when they entered a dark cave, and he was flung into an enormous cauldron full of hot water. Bones and hair, flakes of skin and other things floated upon the steaming surface. The rim of the mighty pot was high above his head, too far for him to reach.

There was a splash beside him and he turned to see Broddgöltur, who was not, to Gunnar's surprise, another child, but an animal. One he recognised. Broddgöltur was a hedgehog, but a hedgehog unlike any he'd ever seen. The creature was bigger than Gunnar, and besides that…

"You can speak!" said Gunnar.

"Um, yes," said Broddgöltur.

"No, I mean … you're a hedgehog, and you can speak."

"Such powers of observation! Listen, we have to escape now, while Grýla is busy taking off her furs, and before this water gets too hot and boils us senseless."

"You're a huge, talking hedgehog."

"Yes, yes. Put that to one side for now. What do you have on your feet?"

"My winter boots."

"Good, then you can safely stand on my spikes."

"What?"

"Here's the plan: I'll roll into a ball, then you stand on me. You should then be able reach the edge of the pot and pull yourself up."

"Can't you just boost me up?"

"What, with these feet and no thumbs? No, I'm likely to drop you, and this must be done quickly before the troll notices. Thank goodness her husband and cat are sleeping. Don't worry, if you're quick – and please be quick – I can hold my breath under the surface. Now, move! Let's get on with it before she turns her attention our way once more."

Broddgöltur curled himself into a large ball, and stuck out his spines to make himself even bigger. Gunnar stepped onto him, and he sank into the grey broth. Bubbles rose to the surface as Gunnar reached up and grabbed the rim of the cauldron with slippery fingers.

He hauled himself up, then twisted around to pull Broddgöltur out after him. They jumped down to the ground and scuttled towards the cave entrance. A loud screech told them that Grýla had finally noticed that her stew was escaping. Gunnar thought they must surely be caught again, but clever Broddgöltur lay on his back, head pointing downhill, and ordered Gunnar to sit on his stomach. They slid rapidly away downhill, the hedgehog's spines acting as runners on the snow.

"Whee!" said Gunnar. "You're like a hedgehog sledge! You're a sledgehog!"

"She'll not catch us now," grinned Broddgöltur. "We're way too fast for her. Gunnar, I can't see very well upside down at this speed, so you'll have to steer. Squeeze my paws to show me which way I need to turn. I'd hate to crash headfirst into a rock or a tree."

Gunnar had the ride of his life, sliding and slipping on the sledgehog down the snow-covered hill towards home. They halted not far from his house, rolling into a snowbank. Gunnar fell from Broddgöltur's furry belly, and helped him to his feet.

"That was wonderful!" he laughed.

"It was rather an exciting ride." Broddgöltur shook snow from between his spines.

"Just wait till Mamma hears about all this."

"Please, Gunnar, you must tell no one of my existence."

"Why not?"

"Because not all humans are kind, like you. Some would want to eat me, and others like me. Others would want to experiment on us, to discover how we can talk. No good can come to my kin by being known to humans. Please keep our existence a secret."

Gunnar agreed, and they parted with a hug. As Gunnar entered the cottage, his Mamma said "You're late, Gunnar!"

"Sorry, Mamma," he said. "I became engrossed by animal tracks."

"See any interesting ones?"

"A sledgehog."

"You mean hedgehog."

Gunnar looked at his mamma, and remembered the sledgehog's words. "Yes," he said. "Just a hedgehog."

Grýla and Leppalúði, the Yule Lads and the Yule Cat are found in Icelandic Christmas folklore. They are mountain-dwelling characters and monsters who visit towns over the Christmas period.

You Better Watch Out

'Twas the night before Christmas, when all through the house not a creature was stirring, not even a mouse. Unless you count me as a creature, of course. Bit of a philosophical question, that. Is Father Christmas a creature, or simply a myth? I'll answer that for you – I'm neither. Rather like Popeye, I am what I am. Only without the spinach and with extra bells.

Yes, I call myself Father Christmas. If you want to call me Santa Claus, go ahead. Pere Noel, fine. Dun Che Lao Ren, I really won't mind. Although, if you insist on Ded Moroz I might put you on my Awkward Sod List. Or the Russian one, depending on where you are.

I have lots of lists. There are the ones that everyone knows, of course: the Naughty List and the Nice List. Then there's a Grumpy List, a Wide-eyed Believers List, and even, if you can believe it, a Horny For Santa List.

KJ was on the Lonely List. She was also, even now in her late thirties, still a Wide-Eyed Believer, which was why I had decided that this year I would make her fondest wish come true. A wish that, emboldened by a bottle of Bailey's, she had revealed to her flatmate Lindsey not three hours ago.

She wanted a man. No, not like that. She wanted a man to love, and one who would love her back, intensely. A soul mate who adored her. Someone who not only did not mind her stretch-marks, but loved them because they were part of her. A man who told her she was beautiful while passing tissues for her streaming, snotty, red-eyed cold. A man who would argue when she needed arguments, cuddle when she needed closeness, and serenade her with songs of honeybees. A man whose heart beat faster whenever she was near, and loved that she cried watching fireworks.

In short, exactly what I had left for her. The man of her dreams. I wish I could see her face in the morning.

*

"Fucking hell, KJ, was that you screeching your head off? What's wrong? What time is it?"

"This is sick! It's vile! Wait, Lindsey, did you do this?

"Do what? I've only just – holy shit! Is that…"

"A severed hand? A real, fleshy severed hand? Yes."

"Bloody hell. Where did you find it?"

"My Christmas sack. Look! It's full of body parts. Arms, legs. Torso. A head."

"A male head. Is there—"

"Trust you. And yes, quite a large one."

"God above. What's that in your other hand?"

"A transparent plastic bag containing 'two fresh eyeballs in their own mucus', according to the label. Who would do this?"

"Fuck knows. It's … wait. Look. There's a note, here. Tied to the big toe."

"What does it say?"

"Some assembly required."

The Nameless Girl

The floorboards pressed hard against the girl's bony hip, and the log that she used as a pillow was cold against her cheek. She still could not remember her name, nor anything before the old man had found her wandering lost and alone in the woods a week ago. She was grateful to him for allowing her to sleep in his kitchen.

She opened her eyes. She felt well-rested, and she was sure it must be way past dawn, yet there was little light in the small room. What illumination there was came not from the orange glow of the fire, which had long since burnt out, nor the dancing yellow of candles. This was a cold blue lustre, as if The Lady of Ice herself had come to visit.

The girl sat up and padded barefoot to the uncurtained window. She shivered, holding her arms tight to her skinny body. The window did not provide the expected view of the rest of the village, green trees and spring flowers. Instead she saw a grey wall. She touched her fingertips to the glass. It was freezing.

"It's snow," the old man said. He sat at the table in the corner, eating a slice of bread.

"But it's Spring," the girl said.

"Nevertheless, the house is buried. Have some bread, then you can help me dig."

It took them all morning, but the old man and the little girl eventually managed to dig a tunnel through the snow from the door to a clear area at the centre of the village. Other tunnels from other houses emerged here too, and the villagers discussed the situation.

"This is the doing of The Lady of Ice," said the old man. "She has hidden the sun behind dark clouds and covered the world with snow."

"I agree, Erik," said a young woman. "It must be her. Long has she wanted permanent winter."

"Freya and Erik have the right of it," said a third villager. "She must have found a way to stop Spring from coming to us."

"But what can we do?" said a fourth. "We shall starve if our crops do not grow."

"Only Father Frost has the power to stop the Lady of Ice," the old man said. "We must ask him for help."

"But his igloo is on the highest peak of the mountain. That is a dangerous trip even in warm weather. In this snow it would mean almost certain death. You'll not catch me going up there."

"Me neither," said Freya. All the other villagers shook their heads, or stared at their feet.

"I would go," said the old man, "but I'm afraid I am too old and slow now. If only I was twenty years younger."

The little girl looked at the faces of the villagers, frightened and cold, and made a decision. "I will go," she said. The villagers all spoke at once.

"But you barely know us."

"You are too young."

"You don't have a hat or mittens."

"You don't even have a warm coat."

"You don't even have a name."

The nameless girl smiled. "I am not afraid," she told them. "My feet are strong and I'm fast and nimble like a mountain goat."

"But you'll freeze up there!" said the old man.

"I will not," the girl said firmly. "I have a warm heart, and it is full of love and gratitude to you for giving me shelter. It will protect me."

The old man looked into her eyes. "Go, child," he said. "I have come to know your good heart since you came to my house, and I trust it."

The villagers gave her their children's winter clothes – a thick coat with a big hood, woollen socks, a cosy scarf, mittens, and good walking boots. She set off, pushing her stick-thin legs through the deep snow at the foot of the mountain. Before she disappeared into the ice-etched clouds she turned to wave back at her new friends.

The old man waved back. "I think I know your name now!" he shouted. She smiled, and turned her face to the winds. She climbed further and higher, never thinking about rest. After a while she could make out the glittering ice on top of the highest peak.

The Lady of Ice saw the little figure in the snow, and awoke her furious whirlwinds to stop her. "Who dares trespass in our domain?" they screamed. "Let us blow her back down the mountain!" The winds threw themselves at the little girl, buffeting her with icy blasts, whirling about her to spin her mind around, but her strong, warm boots kept her securely on the right path. She huddled into her warm coat and bravely trudged ever upwards, her strong warm heart never giving into fatigue or fear. The whirlwinds tired, and one after the other fell to the ground, gasping for breath. "She is too strong for us," they said. "We must call upon our sisters for help."

The Lady of Ice frowned at the little figure in the snow, and awoke her angry blizzards. "She will pay for her temerity!" they howled. "We shall freeze her very heart!" The blizzards threw themselves at the little girl, driving needles of ice at her face, but her thick hood and woollen mittens kept her skin warm and dry. She huddled into her warm coat and bravely trudged ever upwards, her strong warm heart never giving into fatigue or fear. The blizzards soon fell to the ground, breathing heavily. "No human has ever overcome us, let alone such a fragile girl," they said. "We must call upon our mother for help."

The Lady of Ice peered at the little figure in the snow, and spoke to her daughters. "When you cannot defeat someone by force, then turn things about. We shall be good to her."

"What do you mean?" asked a whirlwind. "To kiss her?"

"To be kind, and polite."

"But how will that help us?" asked a blizzard.

"She will think us friends, and will not suspect us of working against her. Rest, my daughters. Leave this to me." The winds settled down, and the blizzards went away.

The girl trudged ever upwards. She was getting close to the mountain top now.

"You look cold, my dear. Can I help?"

The girl turned to see a beautiful woman in a sparkling white gown, with long white hair and a crown of icy diamonds.

"I am going to ask Father Frost for help," she said, "but thank you for your concern."

"But you look frozen," said the woman, concern in her voice. "Here, I have hot chocolate – why not sit for just five minutes and warm your insides?"

The mug in the woman's hands steamed in the chill air, and the girl could smell the tantalising sweet scent of chocolate. She glanced up at the summit. She was so near, with no more than an hour's walk left. She could spare five minutes.

She sat on a snowbank, and clutched the hot mug that the kind woman gave her. The chocolate was delicious. It bathed her tongue in sweet warmth, and made her stomach feel cosy. The woman began to sing as the girl drank, an old lullaby from before time began. The girl closed her eyes, just for a moment. She began to snore, and the mug of chocolate spilled into the white snow.

The Lady of Ice grinned. "Sleep, little girl. May you sleep forever." She left the sleeping girl on the snowy hill, and flew away to tell her daughters how well her deception had worked. The nameless girl slept on. Her pink cheeks turned red, then blue, then yellow. Her heart slowed and began to freeze.

The snow by her feet stirred, and a small hole appeared. A tiny furred head with shiny black eyes peered out at the girl. The mouse shook snow from its brown face and squeaked loudly. "Someone is in trouble!" it cried. "Help!"

More holes appeared. A tangle of mice emerged and ran to the little girl, and began to massage her feet and hands. The creatures were so tiny that their ministrations made little difference, so they set up a loud chorus of piping squeaks. "Help! Help!"

Larger holes opened in the snow, and rabbits appeared. Squirrels descended from the snow-laden pines. A fox, as white as the snow beneath it, joined the other animals with no thought of attacking them. Soon, the nameless girl was covered with a mass of wriggling brown and white fur. Her cheeks became pink again, and she opened her eyes.

"Hurray!" squeaked the mice and squirrels.

"Hurray!" purred the rabbits.

"Yo," said the fox, laconically.

The girl thanked her new friends for saving her life, and told them where she was going, and why.

"Then we shall come with you," said the brown mouse, "for we will also suffer from this never-ending winter." He turned to the other animals. "Who will go up the mountain with the nameless girl to end winter?"

"We will!" squeaked the other mice.

"And us!" purred the rabbits.

"Yo," said the fox.

And so the animals flocked around the girl as she climbed the rest of the way to Father Frost's igloo on the top of the mountain. Several reindeer stood about it, pushing their noses into the snow, or rubbing their antlers against a few stunted pines. The girl was surprised at the size of the igloo. It towered above her head, though the entrance was a normal-sized human door. She knocked on it, more than a few times, but there was no answer.

"Harumph." One of the reindeer raised its antlered head. "You can just go in, you know," it said. "Father Frost never locks his door."

"Thank you," the girl said.

"Harumph," the reindeer replied, returning to its search beneath the carpet of white for a little scrubby grass.

The girl opened the door and stepped inside, followed by her animal friends. They walked, scurried and hopped along a glittering ice corridor which led to a vast crystal hall. There in the centre, on an exquisitely beautiful, brightly-painted, carved wooden throne, sprawled Father Frost. He was dressed in a bright red robe trimmed with white. He was fast asleep, snoring and drooling into his luxurious white beard.

Two squirrels jumped into his lap and tickled his face with their furry tails. A mighty sneeze echoed about the vast chamber, and the girl and her friends froze with fear. Father Frost opened his blue eyes and regarded his visitors. He smiled, and the hall lit up. "Ho ho ho! What are you all doing here, little friends?" He sneezed again, and the squirrels jumped down from his lap.

"The Lady of Ice!" squeaked the mice and squirrels.

"She stopped Spring!" snuffled the rabbits.

"Bless you," said the fox.

The little girl explained everything, and Father Frost's friendly smile turned into a frown. "So that was why she visited me, and brought me a mug of hot chocolate. Not to be friendly, but to make me sleep while she stopped Spring. She thought she could overcome me and stay on Earth forever … but she did not reckon with your brave, warm heart, my girl."

He blew on a silver whistle, and from alcoves all about the hall a horde of tiny people, no more than a foot tall, appeared. He ordered his elves to go and find the Lady of Ice, and to lock her down in the cellar until next year. He also told them to clear the clouds from the skies, so that the sun could finally melt the snow.

"Ho ho ho!" Father Frost laughed. "Thank you for your help, my friends. I would like to reward you with presents for your good intentions and actions. Is there anything you'd like?"

"Warmth," squeaked the mice.

"Food," hummed the rabbits.

"A friend," said the fox.

"A name," said the girl.

"Warmth and food, you shall have," said Father Frost, "and love you shall find, fox." He turned to the girl. "You already have a name," he said. "It is waiting for you down in the village."

When they left the igloo the sky was blue, the sun was shining, and the soft snow had started to melt. The way back down the mountain was much easier. The girl's new animal friends promised to help any time she might need them, and left her to complete the journey on her own.

The people of the village cheered her return, and gave her snowdrops and hugs. The old man put his arm around the girl's shoulders and led her back to his house.

"Father Frost said that you had my name," she told him.

"Father Frost knows everything," he said. "Come inside and get warm. Welcome home, Hope."

About Michael Wombat

A Yorkshireman living in the rural green hills of Lancashire, Michael Wombat is a man of huge beard. He has a penchant for good single-malts, inept football teams, big daft dogs and the diary of Mr. Samuel Pepys. Abducted by pirates at the age of twelve he quickly rose to captain the feared privateer 'The Mrs. Nesbitt' and terrorised the Skull Coast throughout his early twenties. Narrowly escaping the Revenue men by dressing as a burlesque dancer, he went on to work successively and successfully as a burlesque dancer, a forester, a busker, and a magic carpet salesman. The fact that he was once one of that forgotten company, the bus conductors, will immediately tell you that he is as old as the hills in which he lives. Nowadays he spends his time writing, telling tall tales in his bio, and pretending to take good photographs.

Twitter:	@wombat37
Instagram:	@numbat37
Patreon:	Wombat37
Facebook:	wombatauthor
Blog:	cubicscats.wordpress.com
Photography:	wombat37.wordpress.com

Printed in Great Britain
by Amazon

69536451R00031